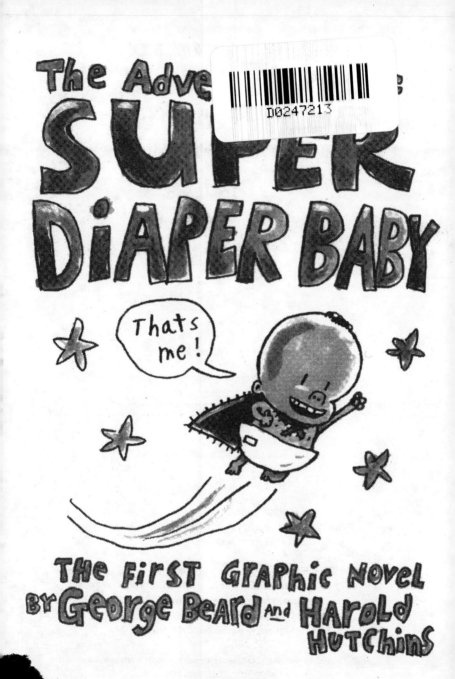

For my mom and Dad
— G.R.B.
To mom and Heidi
— H.M.H.

Scholastic Children's Books,
Euston House, 24 Eversholt Street,
London, NW1 1DB, UK
a division of Scholastic Ltd
London ~ New York ~ Toronto ~ Sydney ~ Auckland
Mexico City ~ New Delhi ~ Hong Kong

First published in the US by Scholastic Inc., 2002
First published in the UK by Scholastic Ltd, 2002

10 digit ISBN 0 439 98161 1
13 digit ISBN 978 0439 98161 3

Printed in the UK by CPI Bookmarque, Croydon, CR0 4TD

12 14 16 18 20 19 17 15 13

Papers used by Scholastic Children's Books are made from wood
grown in sustainable forests.

George and Harold were Bummed.

Why can't we make a comic Book About Captain Underpants?

Yeah — He's A good citizen!

Then They got a great idea!

Hey, Let's make up a _new_ Super Hero And write A comic About him!

OK.

So they went home and got to work.

The next day they turned in their 100-Page "Essay"

What the---

SUPER DIAPER BABY

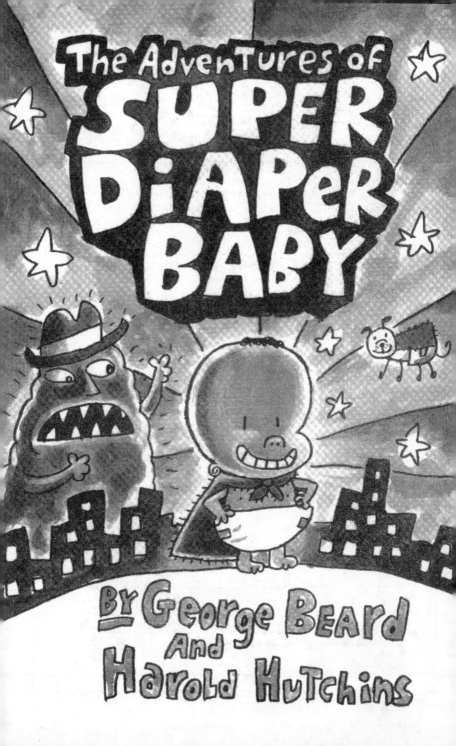

# Chapters

# The Advenchers of ☆SUPER☆ DiAPer BABY

## CHAPTER 1
### "A Hero is Born"

10

But what Mr and Mrs Hoskins Dident know was that there new Baby would have a Job...As A **SuperHero!**

Delivery Room

weee

But... Before we can tell you that story, we Have to tell you **This Story.**

This is Deputy Dangerous and Danger DOG. Deputy Dangerous is the one on The LeFt with the cowBoy Hat and the aposible thumbs. DangeR Dog is the one on the right with the Tail and the Flea problem.

Remember That now.

EVIL PLANS

To secret LABratory

13

14

15

17

19

Haw Haw Haw!
SPLASH
GLUB GLUB GLUB GLUB GLUB GLUB
What the-
KA-POW

Hey You stupid Baby! You drank all my super-power juice! —Give it to me NOW!!!

Uh oh...

# WARNING

THE following pages contains scenes showing A baby beating up a ~~bad~~ bad guy.

Get ready to be OFFended......

Graphic violins

# FLIP-O-RAMA 1

## (pages 25 and 27)

Remember, flip only Page 25. while you are fliping, be shure you can see the pitcher on Page 25 And the one on Page 27.

IF you flip Quickly, the two pitchers will start to look like one Animated pitcher.

Don't forget to add your own sound Affecks

Left Hand Here

take this!

right
Thumb
Here

take this!

# FLIP·O·RAMA 2

## ( pages **29** and **31** )

Remember, flip <u>on</u>ly page 29. while you are fliping, be shure you can see the pitcher on page 29 <u>And</u> the one on page 31.

IF you flip quickly, the two pitchers will start to look like <u>one</u> animated pitcher.

Don't forget to add your own sound affecks

LeFt Hand Here

... And that!

Right thumB Here

... And that!

# FLIP-O-RAMA 3

## (pages 33 and 35.)

Remember, FLip ONly page 33. While you are FLiping, be shure you can see the Pitcher on page 33 and ~~page~~ Page 35.

IF you FLip Quickly, the two pitchers will start to Look Like yadda yadda yadda.

Don't Forget to skip these pages without reading them.

Left Hand Here

... And some of these!

Right
thumb
Here

... And some of these!

36

Ha-Ha. I hope Theres no hard Feelings About my little spanking Acksident. Ha-ha.

FLIP. -O- RAMA 4

HEY!

Left Hand Here

ALL is Forgiven

RiGhT
Thum
Here

ALL is Forgiven

42

44

Lookit! I made a crib that will Transfer all of that babys super Powers to me!
At midnight tonight, this Heat seaking dish will ZAP Super Diaper Babys Powers!
Then his Powers will be beamed by satelite into my new helmet. Then I will GET all of his super Powers.
SATELITE
Heat seaking DISH
Trans-Fer Helmet
ZAP
DANGER CRIB 2000TM
BABY
ME
TRANSFER HELMET
Then I will RuLe The --- HEY!
WAKE UP!

48

But at that very moment The poop was Being Beamed to a satelite.

ZING

SATELIT

And soon it was Beamed Back to earth...

SATELITE

ZANG

...Right to Deputy Dangerouses Transfer helmet.

ZONG

TRANSFER HELMET

Any second now...

50

---Aw Maaaaan!!!

Right
thumB
Here

---Aw Maaaaan!!!

# SUPER DIAPER ★BABY★

## CHAPTER 3
### Dial "R" For "Revenge."

58

When they got back to there Labratory, Deputy Dangerous began making a all-new invention.

60

62

63

Who's Afraid of
the Big, Bad
Bug?

Right
Thumb
here

who's Afraid of
the Big, Bad
Bug?

# FLIP-O-RAMA 7

## (pages **73** and **75**.)

Remember, flip only page 73. while you are fliping, be shure to blah, blah, blah. You're not really reading this page, are you?

well, since your here anyway, how about a gross joke? Q: What's the difference between boogers and broccoli?

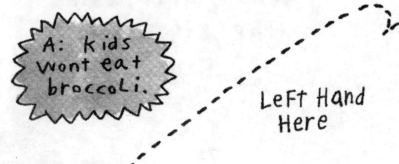

A: kids wont eat broccoli.

Left Hand Here

ALL Shook up!!!

Right
thumb
here

ALL Shook up!!!

# FLIP-O-RAMA 8

## (Pages 77 and 79.)

Remember, Flip only page 77. You know, since nobody reads these pages, we figured they'd be a good place to insert subliminimal messages:

Think for yourself. Question Authority. Read banned books! Kids have the same constitutional rights as grown-ups!!!

Don't forget to boycott standardized testing!!!

Left Hand Here

Watch out, BiLLy!!!

Right Thumb Here

Watch out, BiLLy!!!

80

81

84

# SUPER DiAPER BABY
★ ★ ★ ★ ★

## Chapter 4
" HOORAY FOR DIAPER DOG "

So Danger Dog flew Billy back to his parents house.

Hey look, it's Safety Dog!

Hooray

Doggy saved me!

Wow

How would you like to live with us?

Hold it right there! I'm the landlord and I don't allow no dogs!!!

How come?

Because he might go pee-pee on the carpet!!!

87

88

89

me punch Poopy man.
No! Wait!

Don't touch him! He has absorbed all the newclear radiation from that Power plant.
You'll get mutated!

91

"Poopy-Puncher"

Right
Thumb
here

"Poopy-Puncher"

Head Banger
Blues

Right
thumb
here

Head Banger
BlueS

FLIP-O-
RAMA 11

Left Hand
Here

Around and Around
they went

Right
thumB
Here

Around and Around
they went

106

# SUPER DiAPER BABY

## CHAPTER 5
"Hapily Ever After"

108

On there way back our Heros stopped at Mars for some refreshments.

Man, these Places are everywhere!

Can I help you?

Yeah, ILL take a Large water... and a Juice box for the Kid.

me Like Juice box.

New! Alien Super-Power Juice

Gives You Super Powers!

Super Power Juice

will There be anything else, Sir?

Hmmm

The LAST
FLIP-O-RAMA

Left Hand
Here

And they all Lived
Hapily ever After

Right
thumb
Here

And they all Lived
Hapily ever After

# HOW 2 DRAW
# SUPER DIAPER BABY

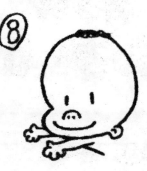

# HOW 2 DRAW
## DiAPer DoG

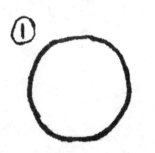

① 

② 

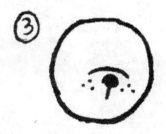

③

④

⑤

⑥

120

# How 2 Draw
# DePuty Doo-Doo

①

②

③

④

⑤

⑥

 7

 8

 9

 10

 11

 12

# HOW 2 DRAW
## The Robo-Ant 2000

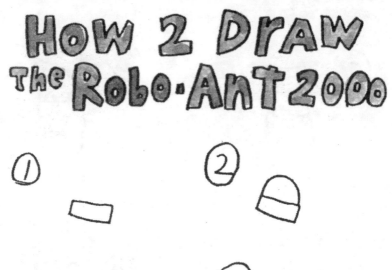

①

②

③

④

⑤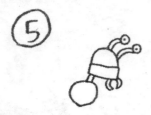

⑥

⑦

⑧

# About the Author and Illustrator

GEORGE BEARD (age 9 ¾) is the co-creator of such wonderful comic book characters as Captain Underpants, Timmy the Talking Toilet and The Amazing Cow Lady.

Besides making comics, George enjoys skateboarding, watching TV, playing video games, pulling pranks and saving the world. His favourite food is chocolate chip cookies.

George lives with his mum and dad, and his two cats, Porky and Buckwheat. He is currently a fourth grader at Jerome Horwitz Elementary School in Piqua, Ohio.

HAROLD HUTCHINS (age 10) has co-written and illustrated more than 30 comic books with his best pal (and next-door neighbour), George Beard.

When he is not making comics, Harold can usually be found drawing or reading comics. He also enjoys skateboarding, playing video games and watching Japanese monster movies. His favourite food is gum.

Harold lives with his mum and his little sister, Heidi. He has five goldfish named Moe, Larry, Curly, Dr Howard and "Superfang."

# We're Sorry !!!

If you were offended by this book, Please send your name and address on a postcard to:

Your name
And Address

"Me was offended by
Super Diaper Baby"
The Publicity Department
Scholastic children's Books
Commonwealth House
1-19 New Oxford Street
London WC1A 1NU

...And we'll send you more offensive stuff.